AZUSA CITY LIBRARY
3 0729 005507106

YOUR MOVE

ILLUSTRATED BY

HARCOURT BRACE & COMPANY
San Diego New York London

Printed in Singapore

At night, when Mom goes to work, I take care of my little brother, Isaac. We do homework or play games or watch TV. But tonight is going to be different.

Tonight we're going out.

We have to make sure Mom's not still waiting at the bus stop, so we play checkers awhile. Every move I make Isaac makes, too. Now that Dad's gone he thinks I'm smarter than anybody. Besides, I'm ten and he's only six.

When we finish two games I thump on our neighbor's wall. We're supposed to do that every night, every hour till bedtime. That way she knows we're all right. She thumps back.

I look over at Isaac in his red sweatshirt. "Let's go," I say. "We have to be back for the next thump or she'll come looking."

"Will we have enough time, James?" Isaac asks me.

"I think so. Whatever it is, it shouldn't take too long." I'm nervous but I try not to let Isaac see.

The K-Bones are waiting at the corner by Rosetti's Pizza Palace. They give me the high K-Bones handshake. Kris and Bones put this crew together, except it's not really a crew. Kris says they're just a bunch of kids who hang out and do cool stuff. Like a club. Tonight I have to prove myself so I can be in their club, too.

STOP
ROSETTIS
Place
OPEN

"How come you brought the little punk along?" Kris asks.

"I told you. I can't leave him alone. What if something happened?"

Kris grins and gives Isaac the K-Bones shake, too. I can tell Isaac likes that.

"So what do I have to do?" I ask.

Kris rattles a can of spray paint. "Just some writing," he says.

I take a deep breath. "You mean tagging?"

Bones shakes his head. "Crews tag. We write." He fakes a punch at Isaac. Isaac likes that, too.

"You know the sign on the 405?" Kris asks me.

I don't know which sign he's talking about, but I nod anyway.

Isaac nods, too, though he knows even less.

"The Snakes put their name on it," Kris says. "You're going up to put our name over theirs."

"Cool," I say, but I'm more nervous than ever.

I hold Isaac's hand as we cross the street; he tries to pull it away.

Now we're walking single file on the narrow road that borders the freeway. Above us traffic roars, loud as a thousand lawn mowers. We can't see it because there's a sloping bank with a wall on top. TV sounds blast from the houses we pass. A dog on a chain barks at us.

Kris stops and points.

High above the freeway, the green sign hangs on its metal pole. Two spotlights shine on it. **ALTA EXIT** it says. Except you can hardly see the words because **SNAKES** is written over them in red curvy letters.

My stomach is acting up. That sign is high. How am I supposed to get to it?

86

"James has to climb *that?*" Isaac asks. He's grabbing at my arms like he wants to keep me back. To tell the truth, I wish he could keep me back. I wish I could slink away. But how can I? I'm here to prove I'm tough enough to be in K-Bones.

We climb the bank, which is covered with scrubby plants.

"But, James . . ." There are tears in Isaac's eyes.

"I'll be OK," I say. "Remember the school picnic when I climbed that cliff?"

"Yeah, but . . ."

Yeah, but . . .

I hand him my jacket. "Hold this."

Bones gives me the can of spray paint, and Kris boosts me up on the wall. It shakes and jolts as the traffic goes by. It's a miracle this wall is still standing. It must be made of steel or something.

"See that electric box halfway up the pole?" Kris shouts. "Stand on that."

I shinny up the pole, slide back, go up again. The pole slams and shakes under my hands. A jumping jackhammer probably feels like this. My foot finds the electric box, and I drag myself onto the platform. I cling to the sign. Wind lifts my hat, balloons my shirt. Below me the chain of headlights goes on forever. I make myself look down and back. Isaac and the K-Bones are a hazy blur.

My fingers are so numb I can't make the paint spray out of the can. When it does the whoosh blows back on me.

But now I'm writing **K-BONES**, looping the letters over the ones already there. I'm doing it left-handed because I'm clinging to the sign with my right arm, and I've got my eyes closed so the paint doesn't get in them. When I reach the **S**, I look. I can read it!

Yeah!

I drop the can on the bank and slide down the pole. Bones and another guy hoist me off the wall. It's a good thing, because I couldn't have jumped. I lean back. The wall is so solid. So is the ground.

Isaac's holding my legs and crying his head off. "I thought you were going to fall," he says.

"Naw." I'm suddenly so cool. I take my bunched-up jacket.

The guys push around me, shouting "Great, man!" and stuff like that.

"We're up!" Kris says. "But we gotta get out of here fast. Somebody could have called us in."

I grab Isaac's hand and we start running. I'm looking back at the sign.

"Do you do this a lot?" I ask Kris, panting out the words because we're running so hard.

He flashes me a grin that I can see clearly in the streetlights.

"Sometimes we play the 'take-it' game. You know, take it from the minimarket, take it from Bates Drugs."

"You mean, *steal?*"

"No, it's a game."

"You're pulling me too fast," Isaac whines, and I slow down a little. I'm not feeling too great about getting him mixed up in this. I should have known the kind of stuff the K-Bones do. I'm not that dumb. Maybe I did know. But I wanted to be in with them.

Suddenly everyone stops.

"Snakes!" one of the K-Bones yells.

The guys in front of us are all wearing black. They're big. Maybe they're even in high school.

"K-Bones rule!" Kris calls out, but his voice is as rattly as the freeway pole.

"Not for long," one of the Snakes says, and I'm thinking, OK, they're going to go right back up that pole and write over what I just wrote. Then the K-Bones will come back and . . .

"Run! Go! They've got a gun!" Bones shouts.

A gun! I've never felt my heart slide around the way it's sliding now.

We're all running. I'm dragging Isaac 'cause he's so slow. The K-Bones are way ahead.

Then I hear a shot. I've heard shots before around our building, and I know how they sound.

Isaac falls, and for an awful minute I think he's been hit. But it's just that I'm pulling him too fast. "Let go of me! Stop!" he yells.

His knees are scraping along the ground and he's screaming his head off but I can't stop. We've got to get away. I glance down. Oh no! The knees have been torn out of his jeans and there's blood. I look back and see the Snakes have disappeared, so I stop.

"Aw, Isey," I say. "I'm sorry. Are you OK?" I crouch down beside him.

That's when he sees the blood, and that's when he *really* starts screaming. "Blood! Blood!" he yells.

I have to almost carry him home, and when we get there Mom and Mrs. Lopez from next door are waiting. Mom's still in her Drew's Cafe uniform.

"You didn't thump, James," Mrs. Lopez says, all mad. "And when I came in you were gone. What are you trying to do? Give me an attack?"

Mom's staring at Isaac's knees. "What happened?"

"He fell down," I say.

"I fell down," Isaac says.

Mom frowns. "I'm not happy about this, James. I *have* to be able to trust you."

She bathes the blood away and puts on antiseptic stuff that stings and makes Isaac yell some more. Mrs. Lopez gets the bandages.

Mom says that from now on she's taking no more chances. Tomorrow she'll put a notice on the supermarket board and have someone stay with us full-time while she's at work. She'll find the money somehow.

"I'd do it myself, but Mr. Lopez likes me with him at night," Mrs. Lopez says.

Mom tells her she understands.

For now, Isaac and I are on our honor. Even so, we have to thump on the wall every half hour.

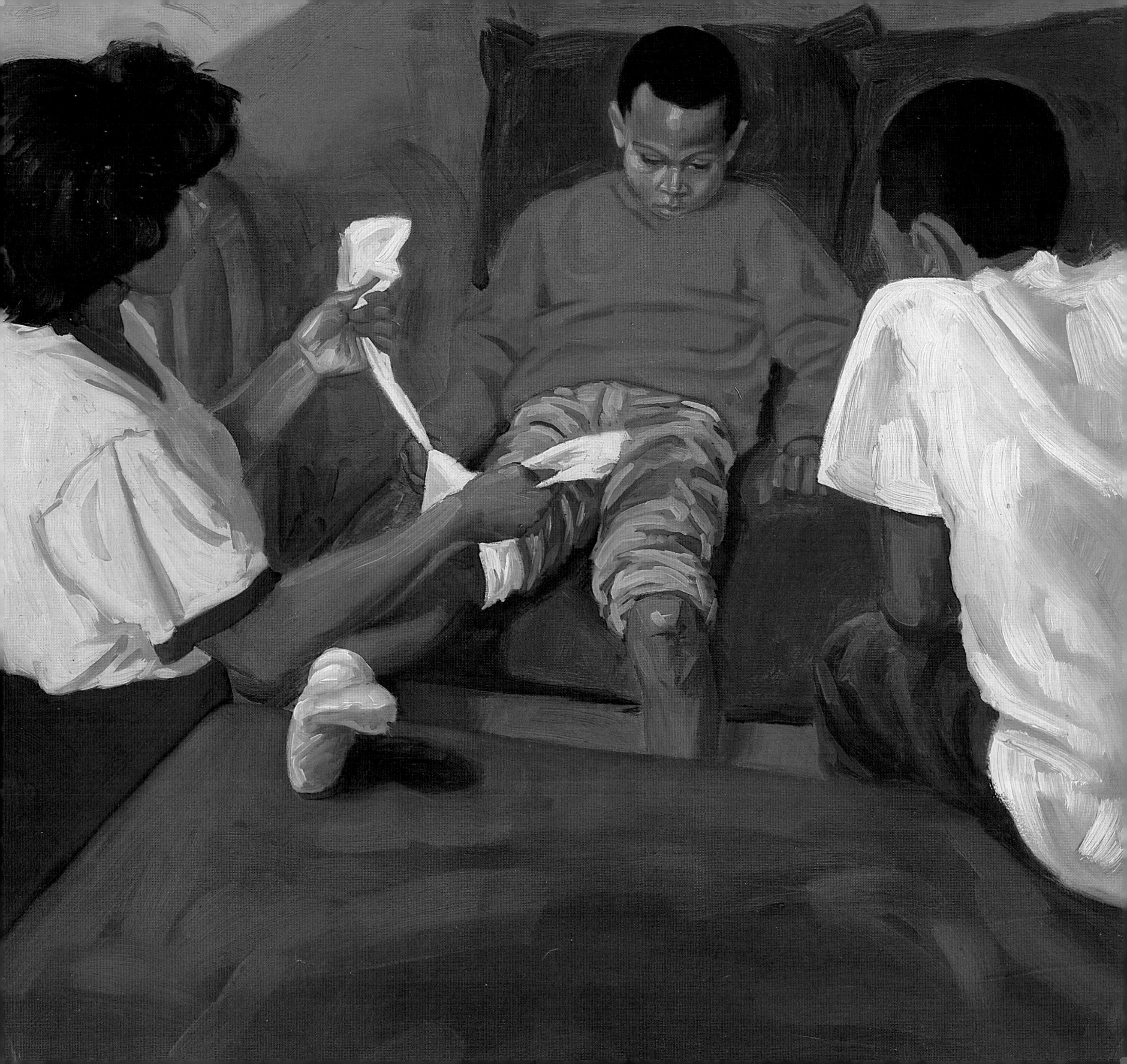

The very next night, we're playing checkers when someone knocks real softly on the door. Through the peephole I see Kris.

I let him in.

He's wearing a brand-new Lakers cap and carrying another.

"How are you doing?" he asks Isaac, staring at the bandages.

"He could have been dead," I say.

Kris grins. "Naw. Those Snakes couldn't hit a brick wall if they had a cannon. When we get a gun . . ." He stops.

When they get a gun! Oh, great! Give me a break, I think.

"Anyway," Kris says. "The K-Bones took a vote. You're in, James. You, too, Isaac, even though you're just a little punk." He takes off the Lakers cap and gives it to me. "We've all got these now," he says. "Club caps."

I turn it in my hand. Club cap. Crew cap. Lifted in a take-it game.

I give it back. "Thanks. But no thanks."

Kris looks at me. It's like he's reading my thoughts. He looks away.

"Well, here's yours." He sets the other cap on the table beside Isaac.

Isaac touches the peak. He loves the Lakers. He wants this cap, I can tell. It's brand, sparkling new, purple and gold. He picks it up, holds it, sighs, and gives it back to Kris. "Thanks. But no thanks," he says.

Kris grabs it from him. "That's what I get for sticking up for you guys." He's really mad. When he slams the door behind him the whole apartment shakes.

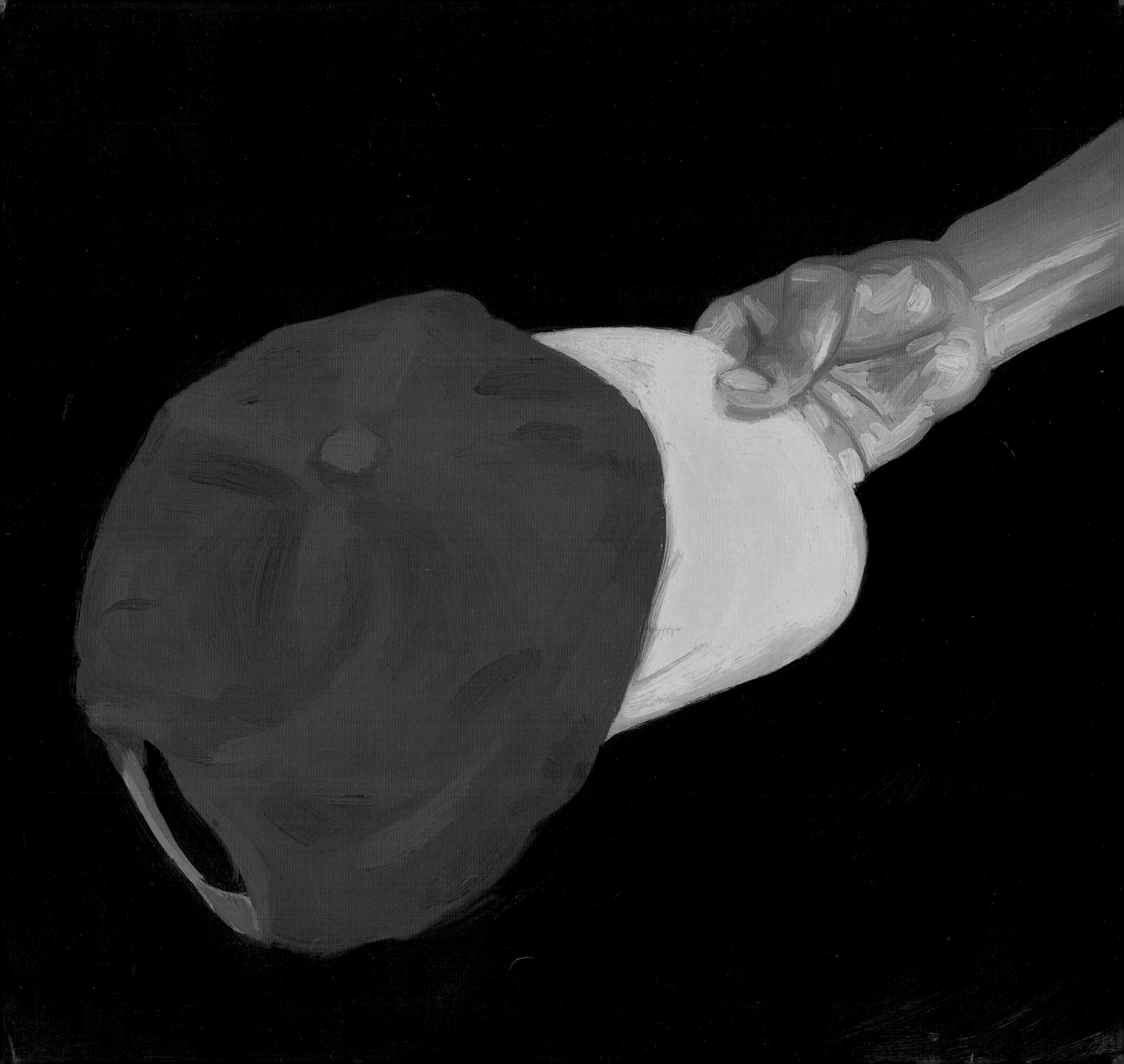

We listen for the gasp of the outside door at the bottom of the stairs, and when we hear it Isaac says: "He's gone." He pushes the checkerboard toward me. "Your move, James."

He watches, then makes the same exact move I make.

I smile. "You're so weird, Isaac," I say.

But it's OK. He's only six. And I'm his brother.

Requests for permission to make copies of any part of the work should be mailed to: Permissions Department, Harcourt Brace & Company, 6277 Sea Harbor Drive, Orlando, Florida 32887-6777.

Library of Congress Cataloging-in-Publication Data
Bunting, Eve, 1928–
Your move/Eve Bunting; illustrated by James Ransome.
p. cm.
Summary: When ten-year-old James' gang initiation endangers his six-year-old brother Isaac, they find the courage to say "Thanks, but no thanks."
ISBN 0-15-200181-6
[1. Brothers—Fiction. 2. Gangs—Fiction.]
I. Ransome, James, ill. II. Title.
PZ7.B91527Yo 1998
[Fic]—dc20 96-18603

First edition F E D C B A

For Diane D'Andrade, who tholes
—E. B.

To the late Christopher Wallace,
A.K.A. Notorious B. I. G., Biggie,
or Biggie Smalls.
You were the . . . BEST!
—J. R.

The illustrations in this book were done in oil paint on Arches watercolor paper.
The display type was set in many different weights of Gill Sans.
The text type was set in Gill Sans Regular.
Color separations by Bright Arts, Ltd., Singapore
Printed and bound by Tien Wah Press, Singapore
This book was printed on totally chlorine-free Nymolla Matte Art paper.
Production supervision by Stanley Redfern
Designed by Camilla Filancia